*There are many versions of this classic
tale. In the tradition of the storyteller,
each one is uniquely different.*

— *Jane Belk Moncure*

Library of Congress Cataloging-in-Publication Data

José, Eduard.
    Cinderella.

    (A Classic tale)
    Translation of: La Cenicienta.
    Summary: In her haste to flee the palace before
the fairy godmother's magic loses effect,
Cinderella leaves behind a glass slipper.
    [1. Fairy tales.   2. Folklore – Germany]
I. Grimm, Jacob, 1785-1863.   II. Grimm,
Wilhelm, 1786-1859.   III. Asensio, Agustí, ill.
IV. Moncure, Jane Belk.   V. Aschenputtel.
VI. Title.   VII. Series.
PZ8.J747Ci   1988   398.2'1'0943   [E]   88-35317
ISBN 0-89565-483-0

© 1988 Parramón Ediciones, S.A.
Printed in Spain by Sirven Gràfic, S.A.
© Alexander Publishers' Marketing
and The Child's World, Inc.: English
edition, 1988.
L.D.: B-44.046-88

THE BROTHERS GRIMM

Cinderella

Illustration: Agustí Asensio
Adaptation: Eduard José

Retold by Jane Belk Moncure

The Child's World, Inc.

Once upon a time in a far away land, there lived a kind and beautiful girl named Ella. Her mother had died, leaving her very sad and lonely. Ella's father was a nobleman who served the king. He was often away from home.

"I cannot leave my daughter alone," he said. So he married a second time. His new wife had two daughters of her own.

Ella welcomed her new family with open arms, for she had a heart full of love for everyone. But the wicked woman and her daughters did not. They were ugly and mean. Most of all, they were jealous of Ella's beauty.

"She may look pretty now," said one of the stepsisters. "But we shall see how pretty she looks when she is doing all our chores."

"That's right," said the other. "We will keep her busy."

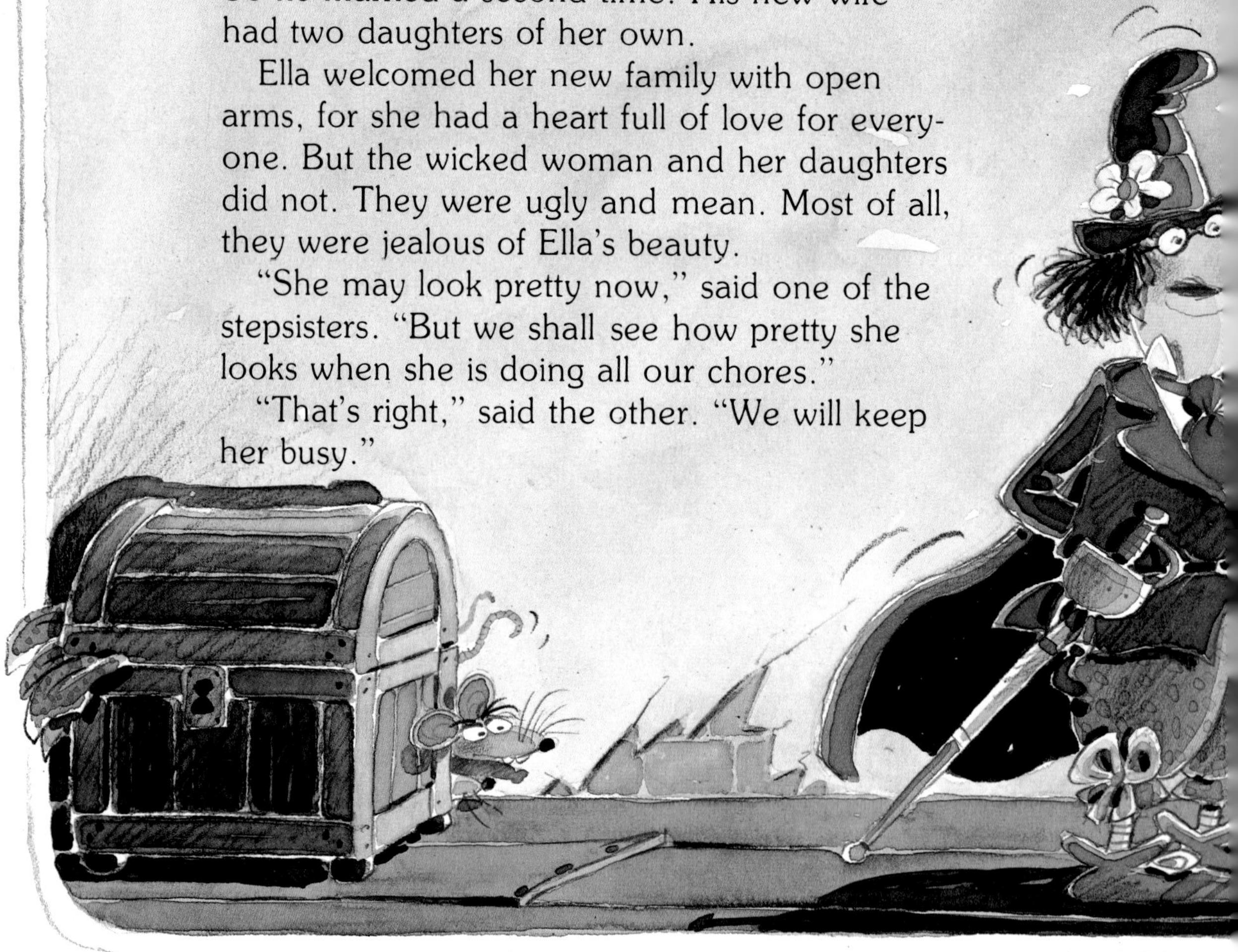

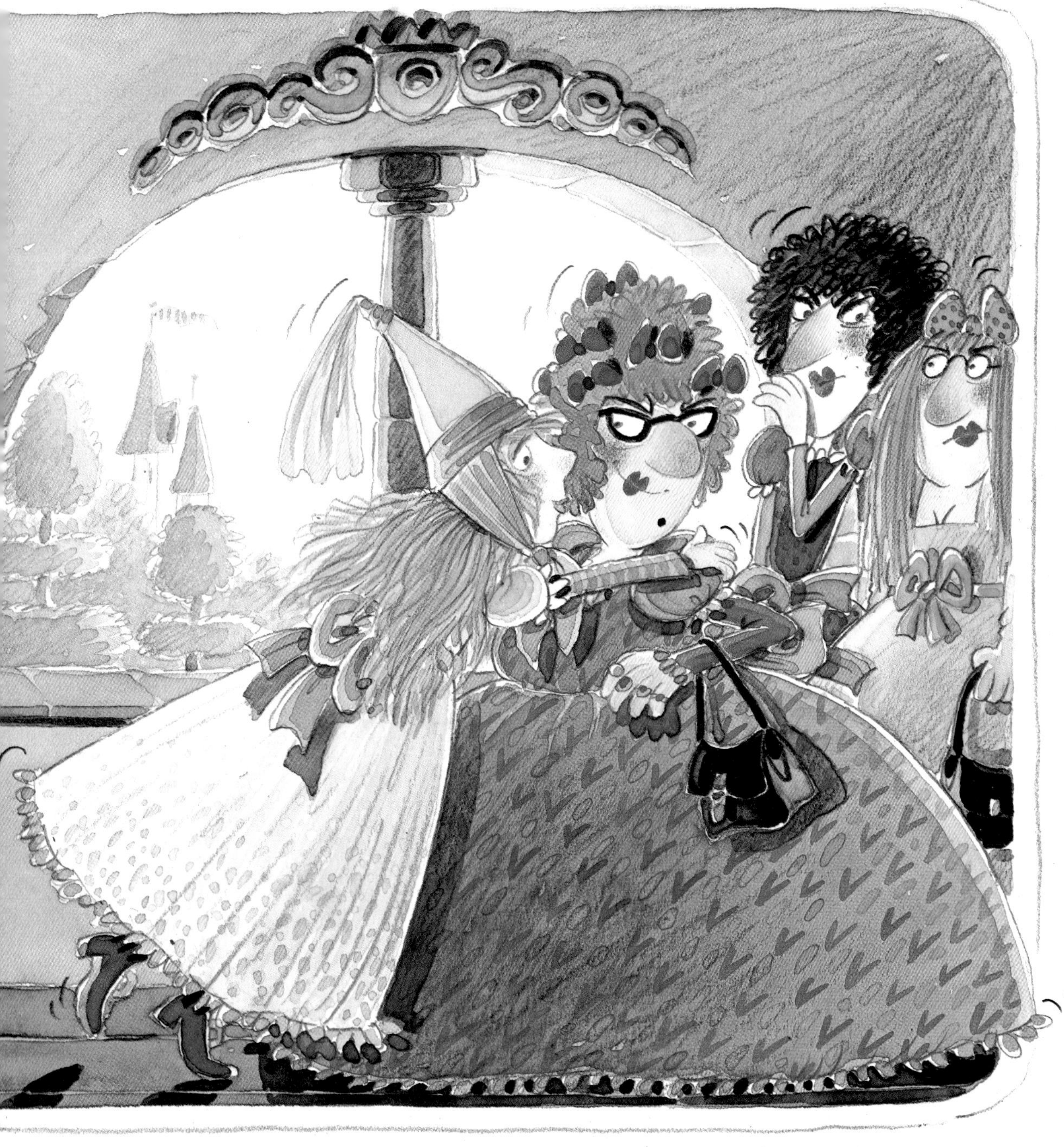

And so they did. The poor girl worked from early morning until late night. She swept the floors, cooked the meals, and washed the clothes. Her stepsisters ate the best foods, bought the best clothes, and went to parties all day long. But poor Ella ate crumbs from the table and dressed in rags.

"Look," her stepmother joked one day. "She spends so much time by the stove that she is covered in cinders."

"Let's call her Cinderella," laughed the elder stepsister.

And so it was that Ella became known as Cinderella. But even her rags did not hide Cinderella's beauty, and her heart was as kind as ever. The tiny mice from the attic and the birds from the forest loved Cinderella.

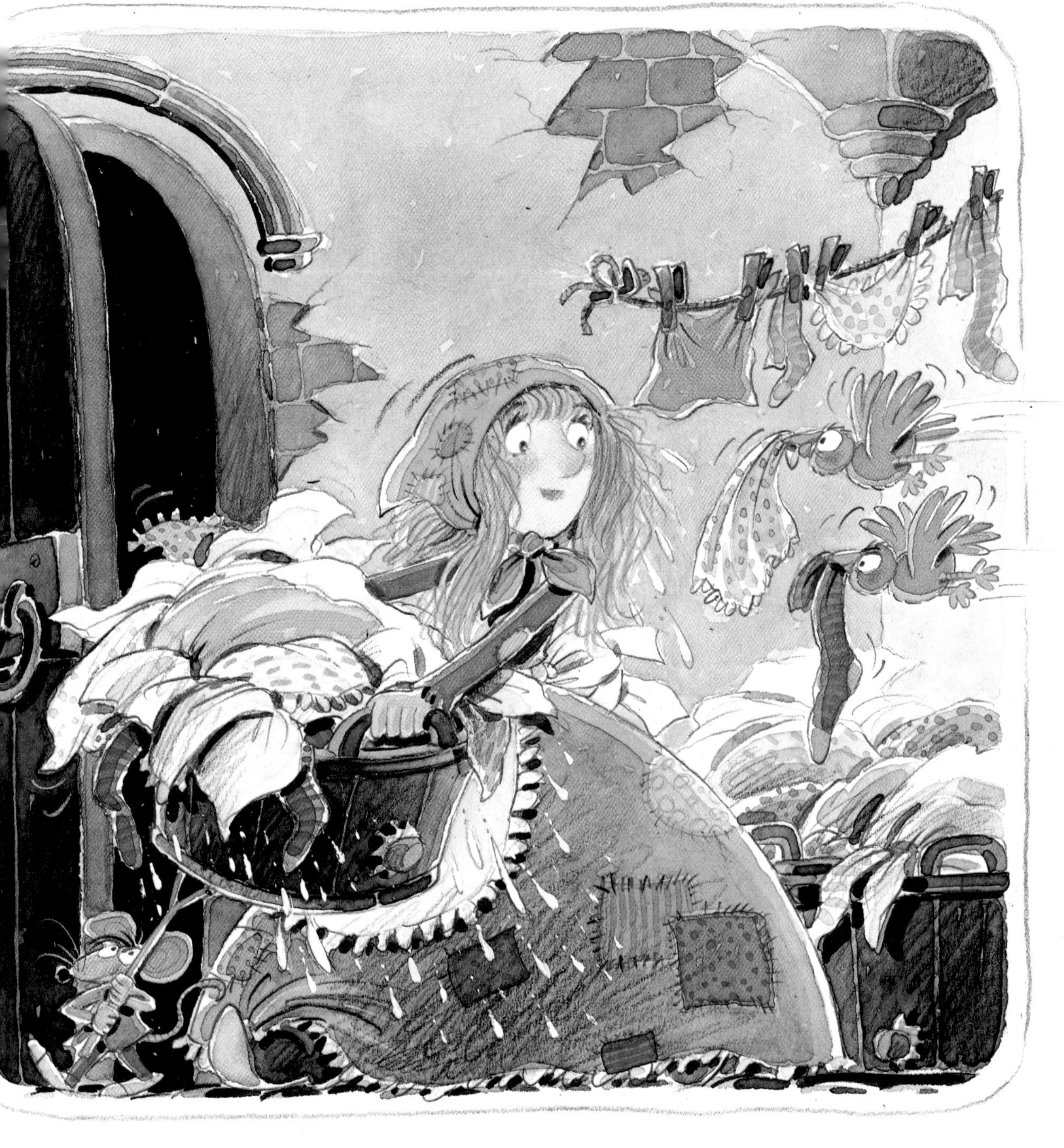

Cinderella was sure that one day the three women would change their minds and treat her as kindly as she treated them. So she kept trying to please them. Yet it seemed the more she did for them, the more they asked of her.

"Cinderella, make my bed!"

"Cinderella, fetch my coat!"

"Cinderella, scrub the floor!"

Every night Cinderella was so weary that she fell into her bed of straw. She would have cried, had it not been for her tiny friends, the birds. They sang to her of joy and hope.

"Perhaps one day things will change," she said.

Yet she had no idea of the surprise that awaited her.

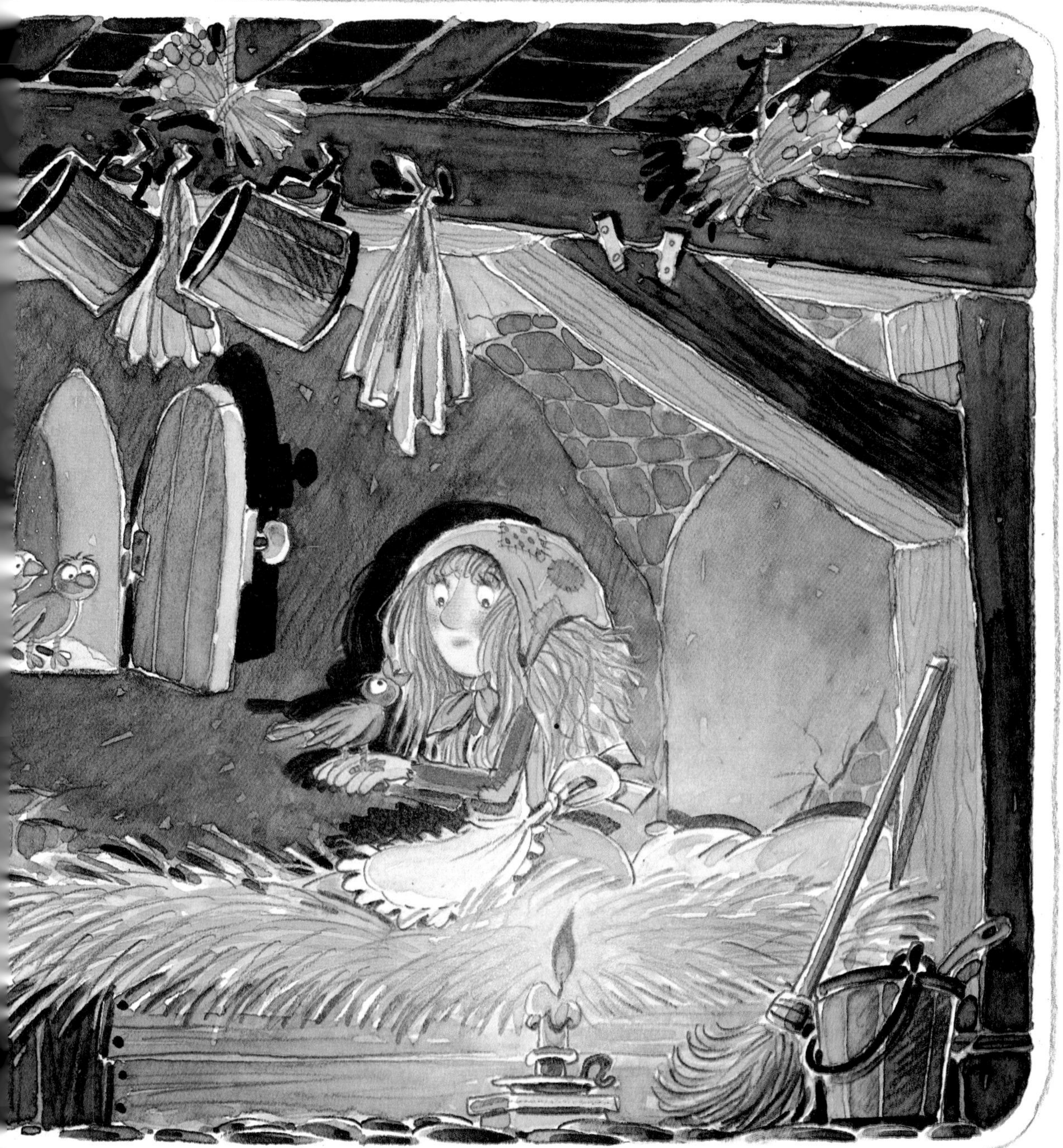

It happened one day that a messenger from the king's palace stood before the nobleman's house.

"Hear ye! Hear ye!" he called. "The king requests your presence at a royal ball tomorrow night. The prince is searching for a kind and loving wife."

"Surely the prince will choose one of my daughters," said the stepmother.

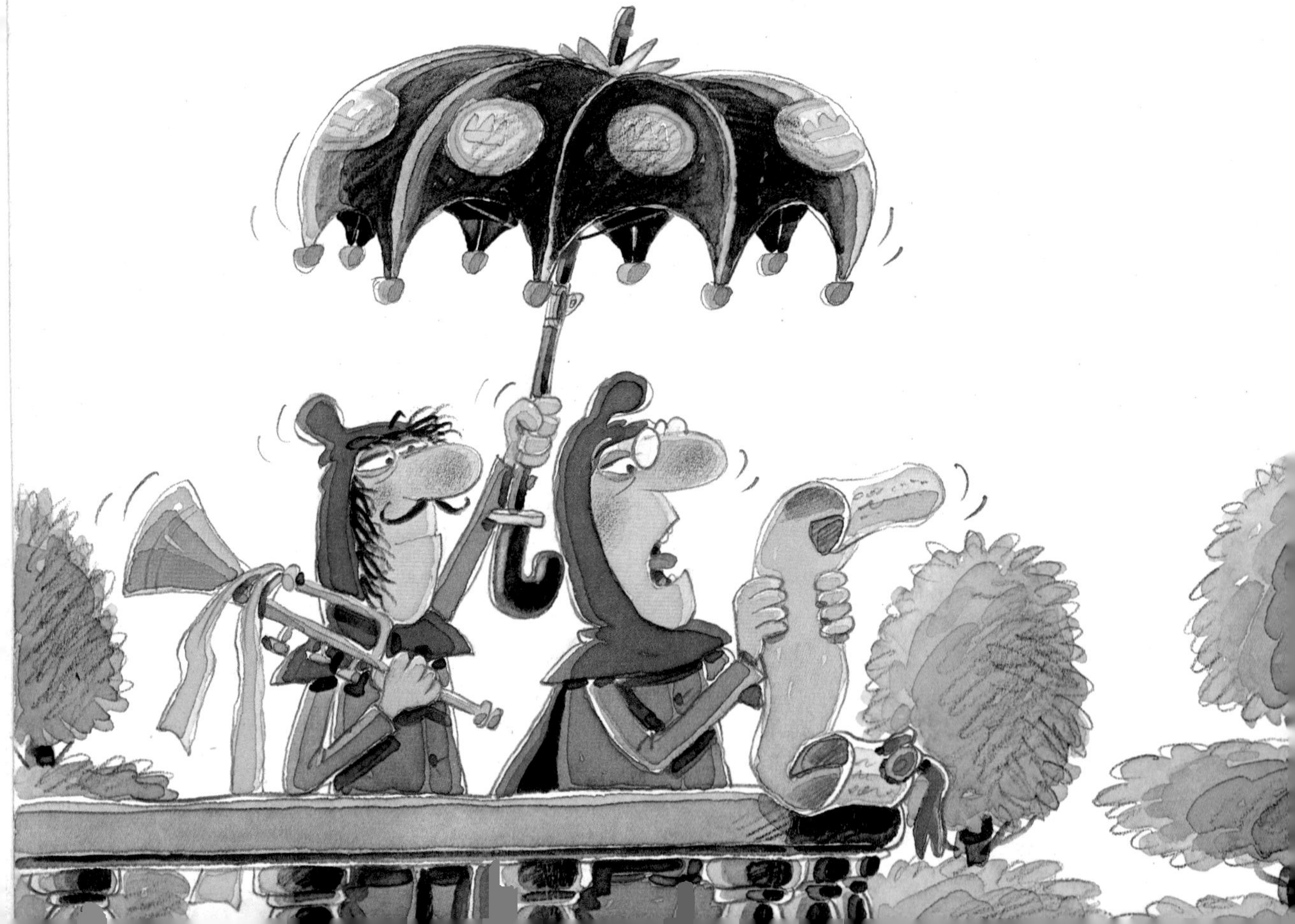

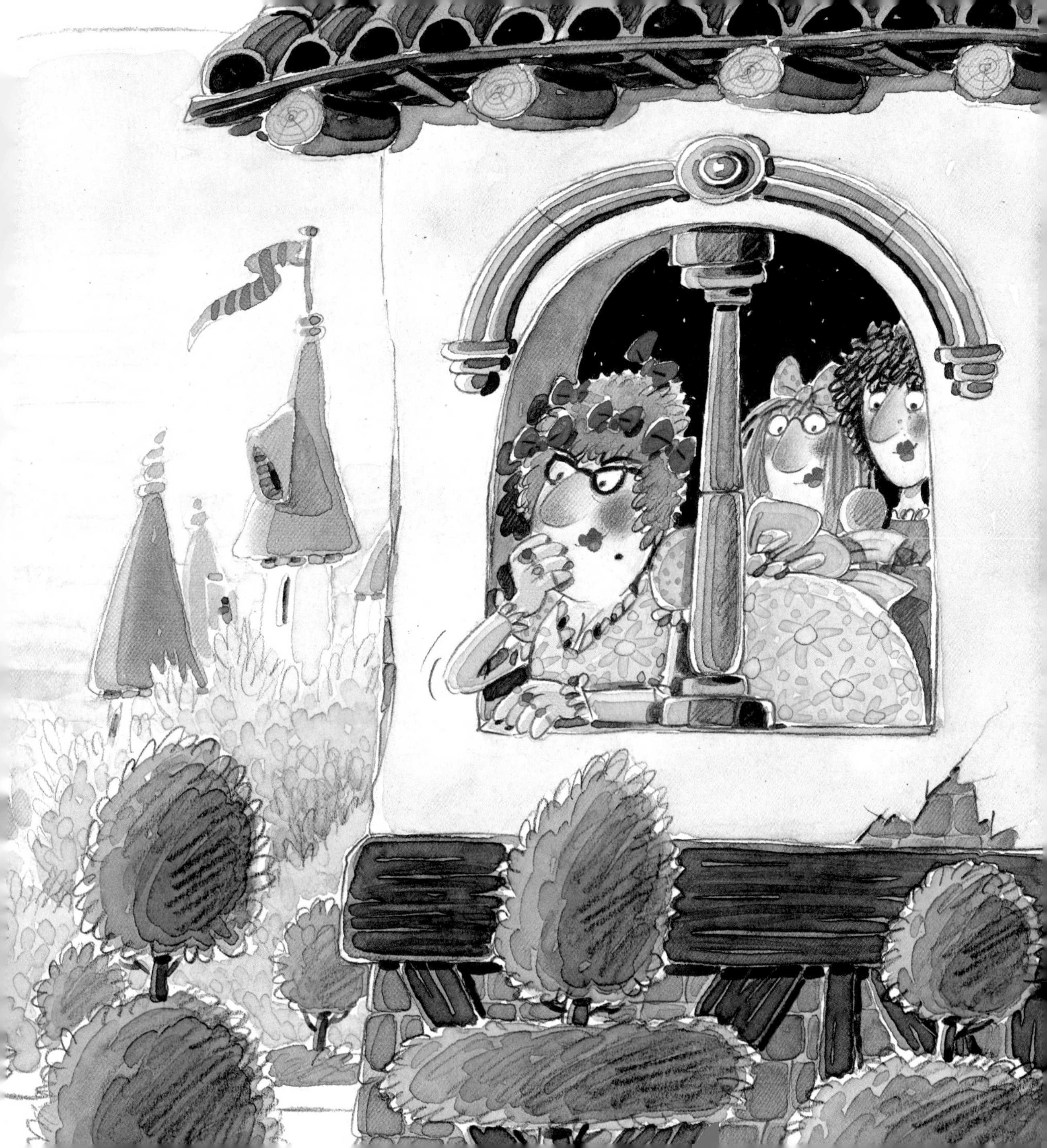

At once the sisters began planning what to wear to the king's ball.

"Sew the buttons on my velvet gown, Cinderella," said one.

"Press my finest lace gown, Cinderella," said the other.

So Cinderella went to work on her step-sisters' beautiful gowns.

"Do you think . . . that is . . . perhaps I could go to the ball with you?" she said.

The three of them roared with laughter. "Everyone at the palace would laugh at a cinder-girl in rags," they said.

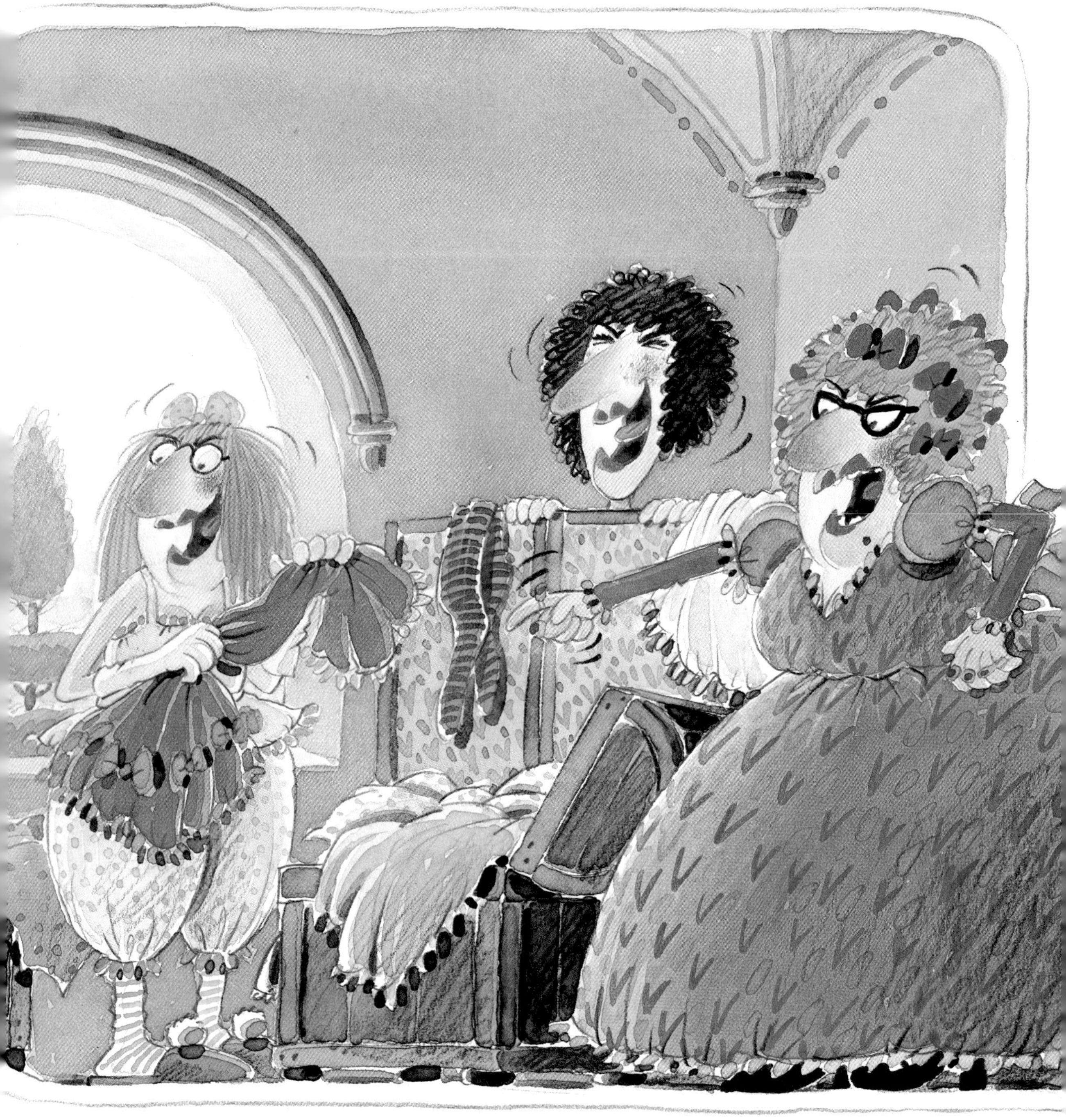

All the next day Cinderella was busy helping her two stepsisters dress for the royal ball.

Although she was brokenhearted that she could not go, she smiled bravely.

At last the three women were ready to leave for the palace. "Lock the door when we leave," called out Cinderella's stepmother. "And I want all these floors washed tonight!"

"When we come home, we'll tell you which of us the prince will marry," said the elder stepsister.

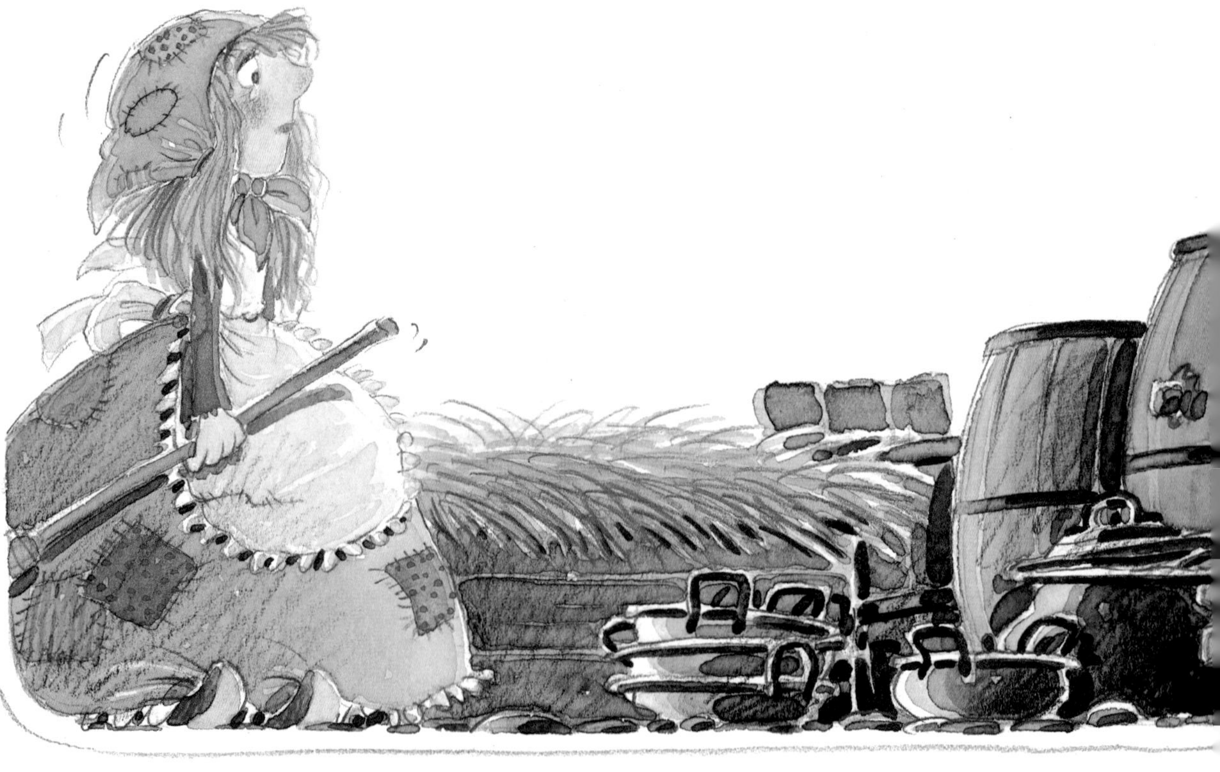

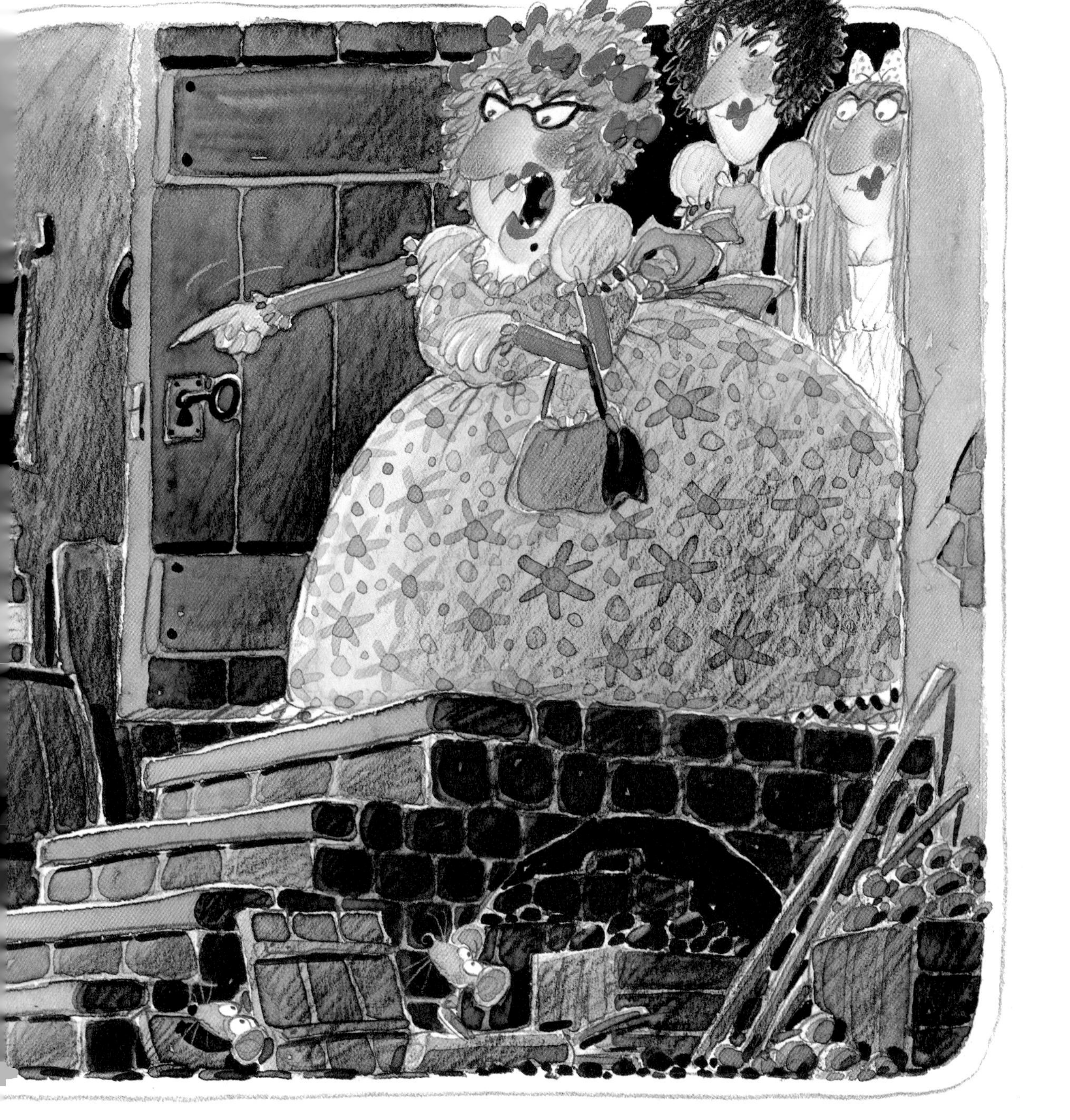

Cinderella said not a word. She held back the tears until the three women were out of sight. Then she ran to the kitchen window. Tears fell from her eyes when she saw the lights of the palace in the distance.

Suddenly the kitchen was filled with light. In the middle of the light, a fairy godmother appeared.

"Do not cry, my dear," she said. "You shall go to the ball! Now, run into the garden and fetch me a pumpkin. Then fetch six mice and a whiskered rat from the barn. Hurry, child!"

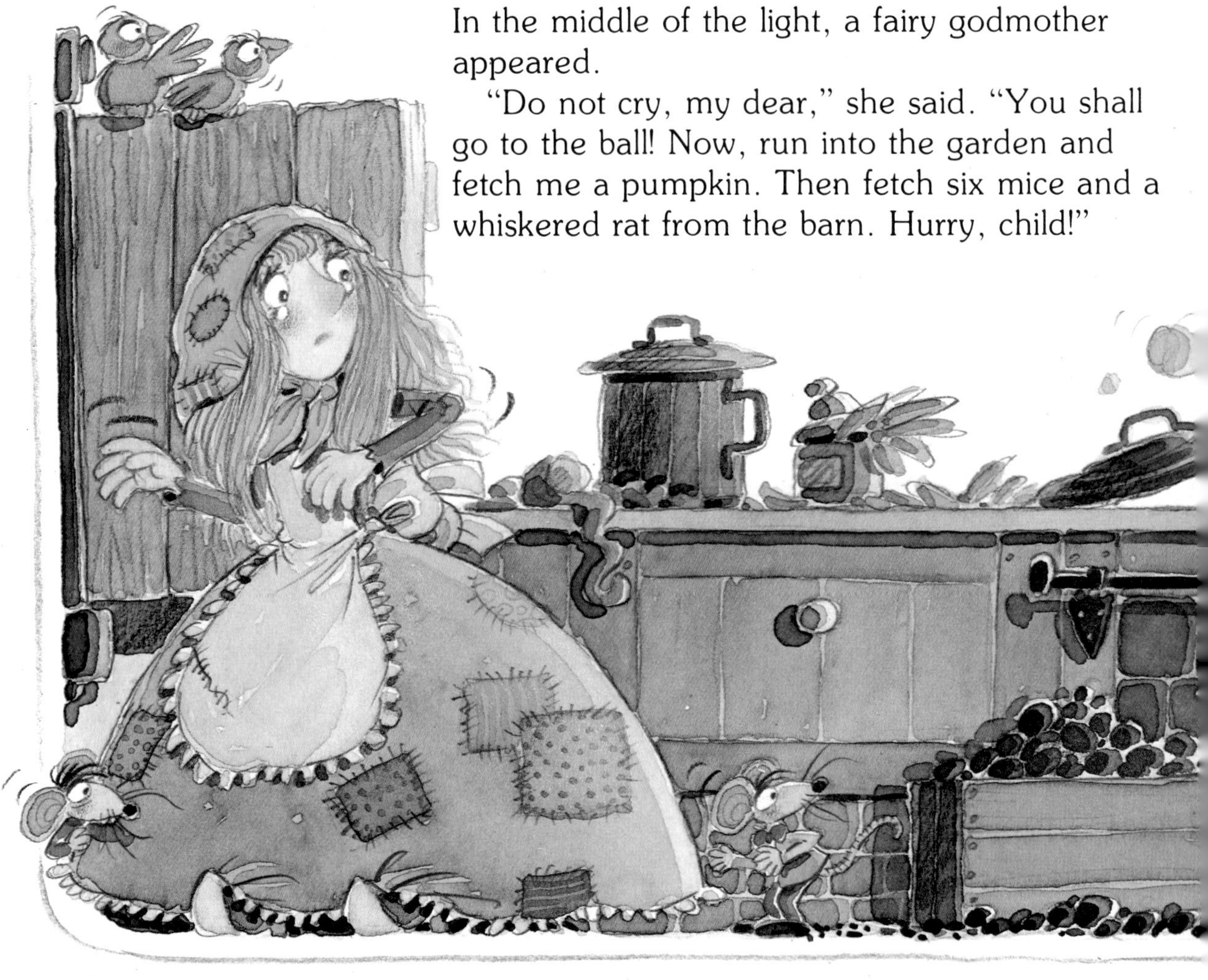

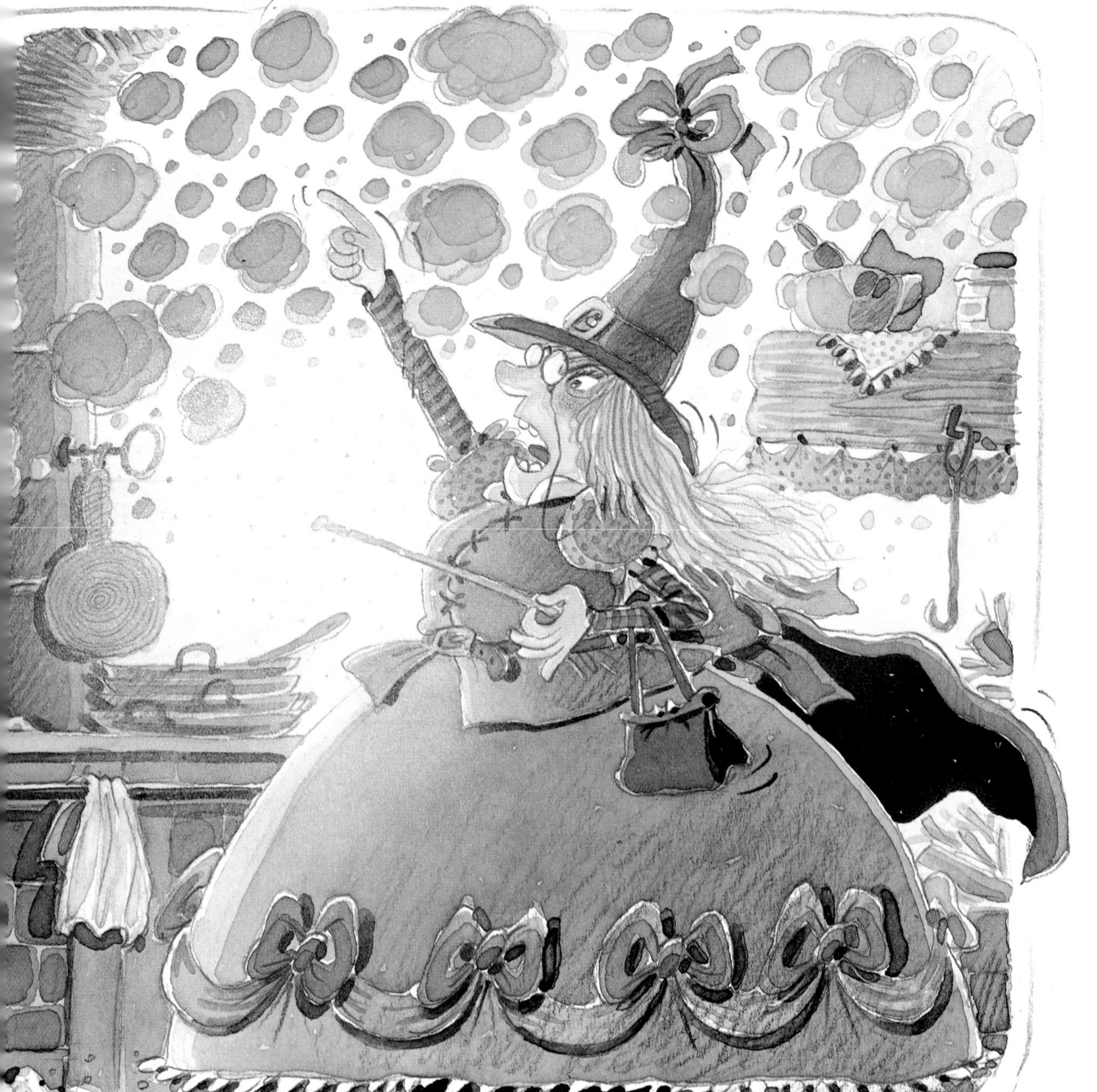

No sooner had Cinderella done as she was told than the fairy godmother waved her magic wand. At once the pumpkin became a golden coach, the mice became prancing horses, and the whiskered rat became a coachman.

With another wave of the wand, the fairy godmother turned Cinderella's rags into a sparkling evening gown. And her wooden shoes became glass slippers.

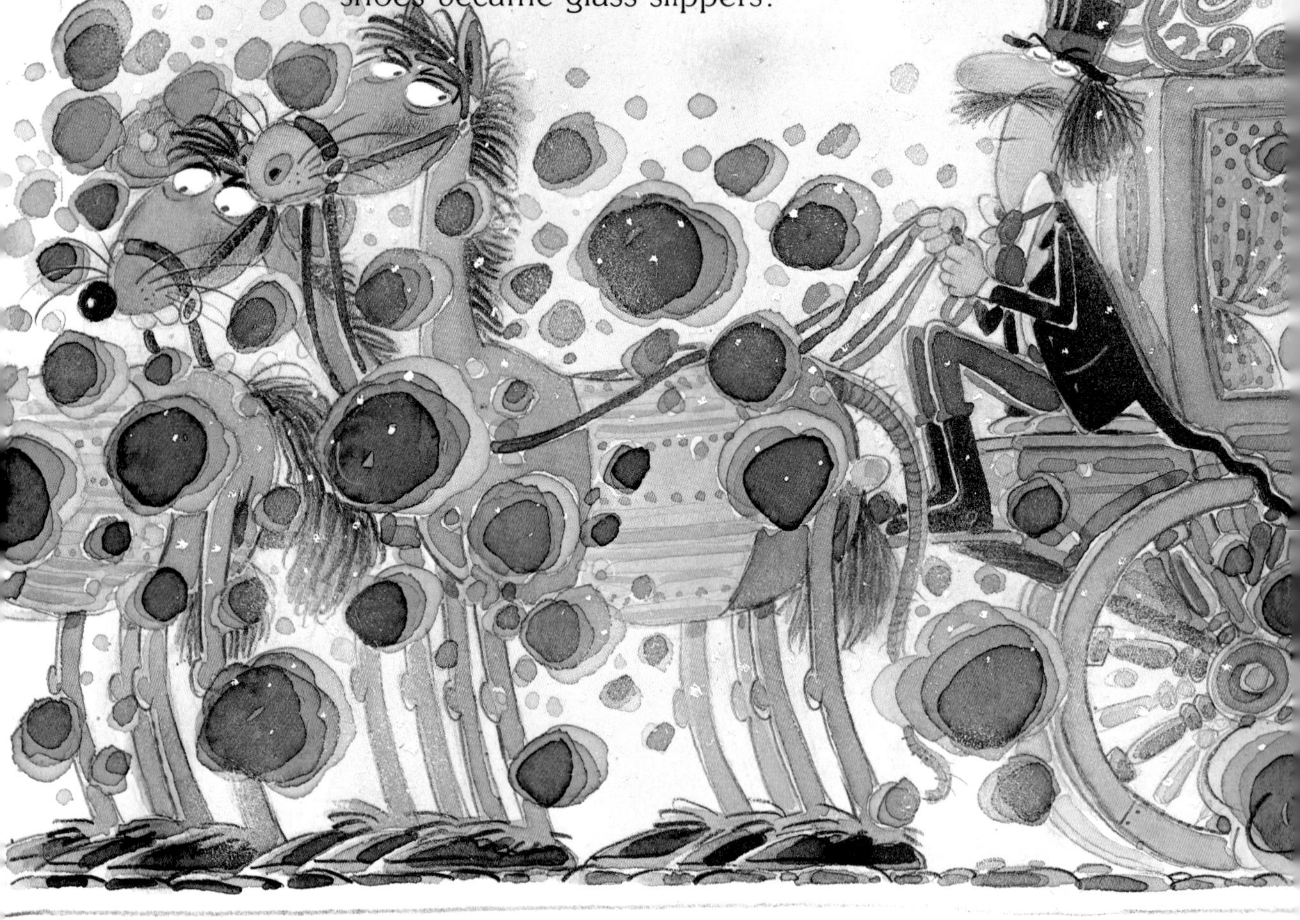

“Now remember, my dear,” said the fairy godmother, “you must leave the ball before the clock strikes twelve. For at midnight the magic spell will be broken.”

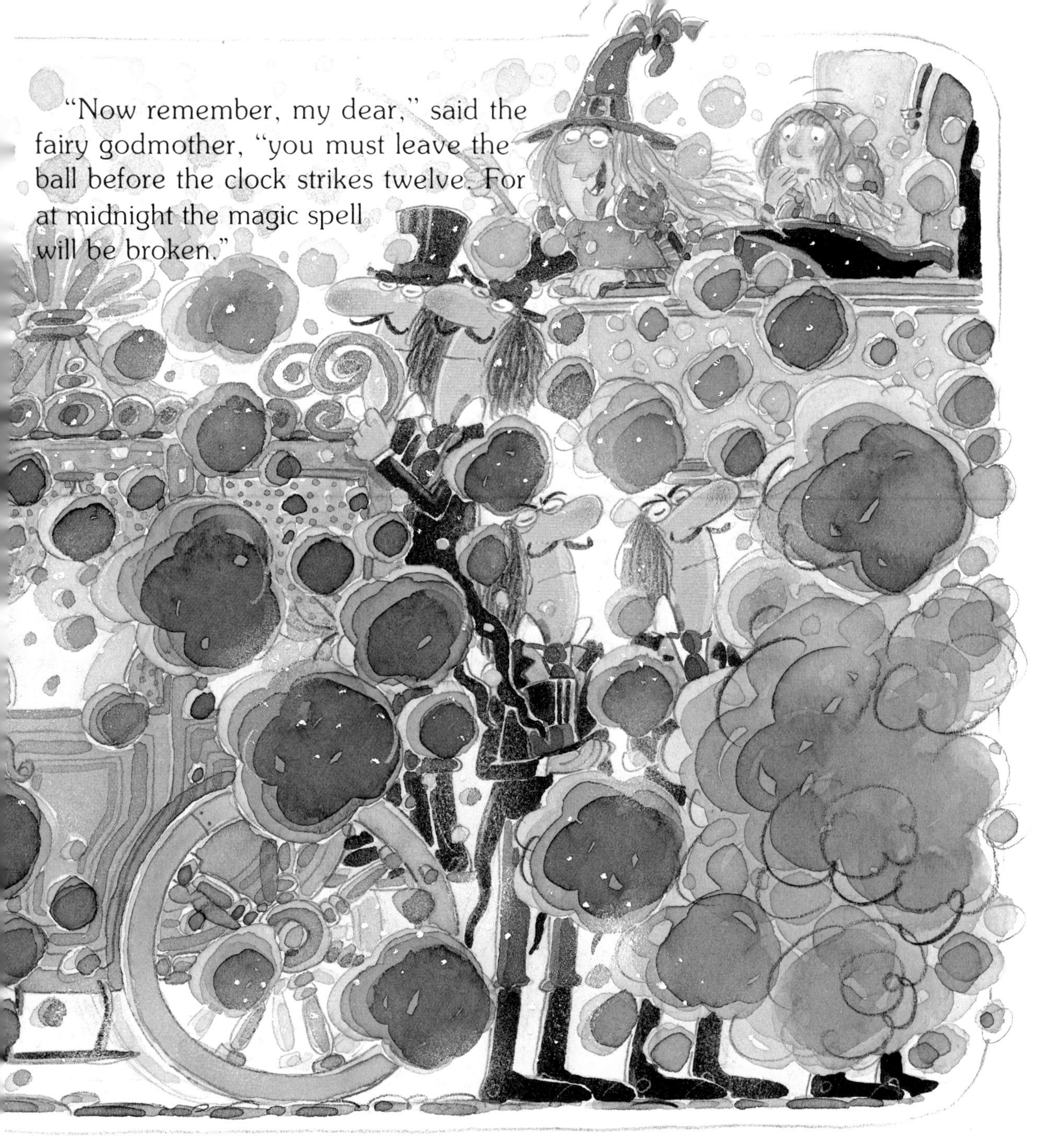

Cinderella promised. She kissed her fairy godmother good-bye and off she went to the palace.

When she arrived at the ball, everyone wondered who the beautiful young woman was. "Surely she is a royal princess," said the queen.

The prince was dazzled by Cinderella's beauty. He danced with her all through the evening and they talked late into the night. Cinderella was overjoyed. She was having such a wonderful time, she forgot all about her promise—until the clock struck twelve!

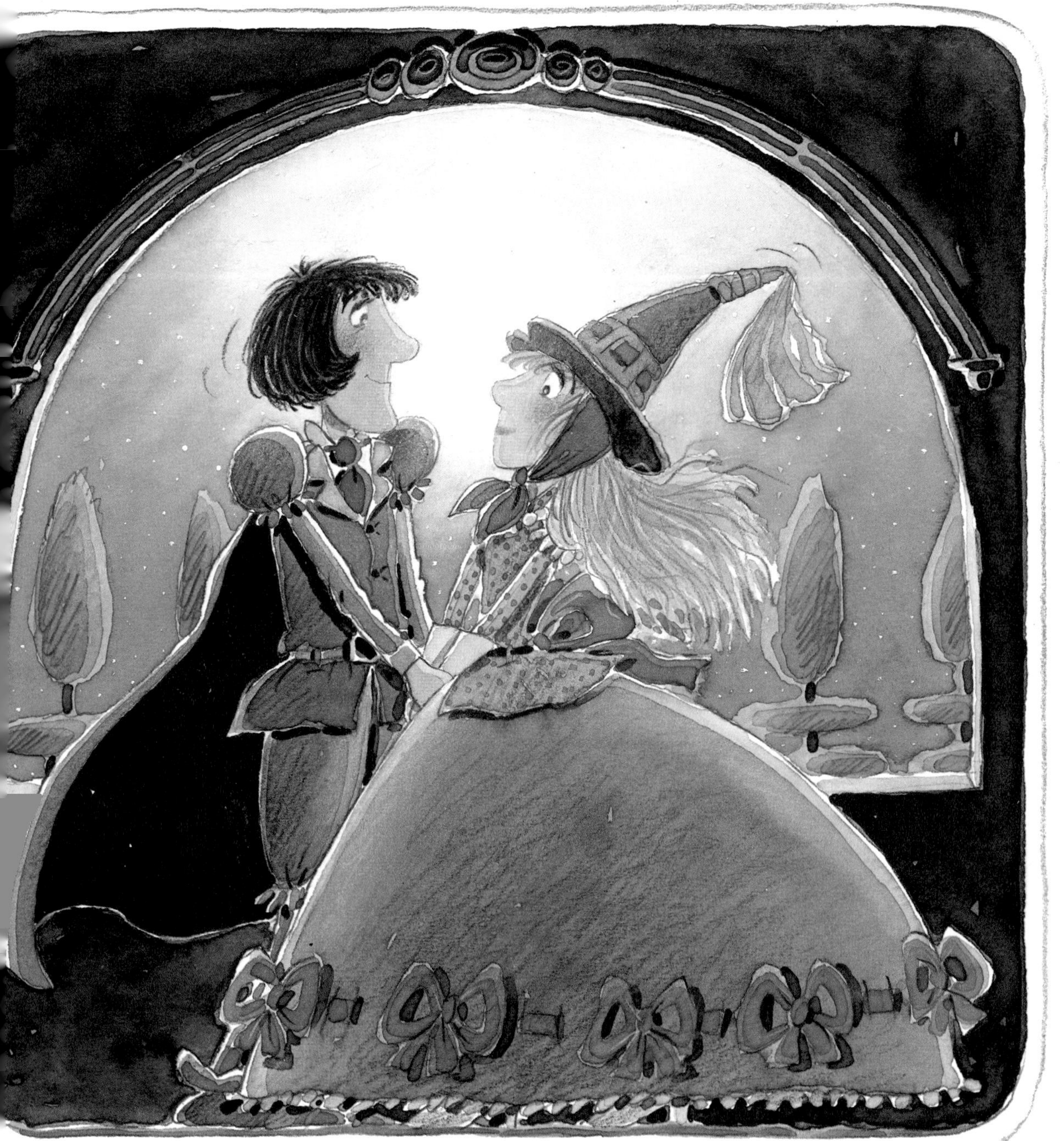

In great haste, she dashed from the palace. She ran down the stairs so fast that one of her glass slippers fell off! But she had no time to turn back for it.

By the time Cinderella reached the road, her coach had turned into a pumpkin. The mice and the whiskered rat had scampered into the field. Cinderella had no choice but to run home.

The poor prince was very confused. He ran out of the palace after her, but she was nowhere to be seen. The prince was heartbroken.

"I must find her!" he cried. Then he saw the tiny glass slipper on the stairs. He had an idea.

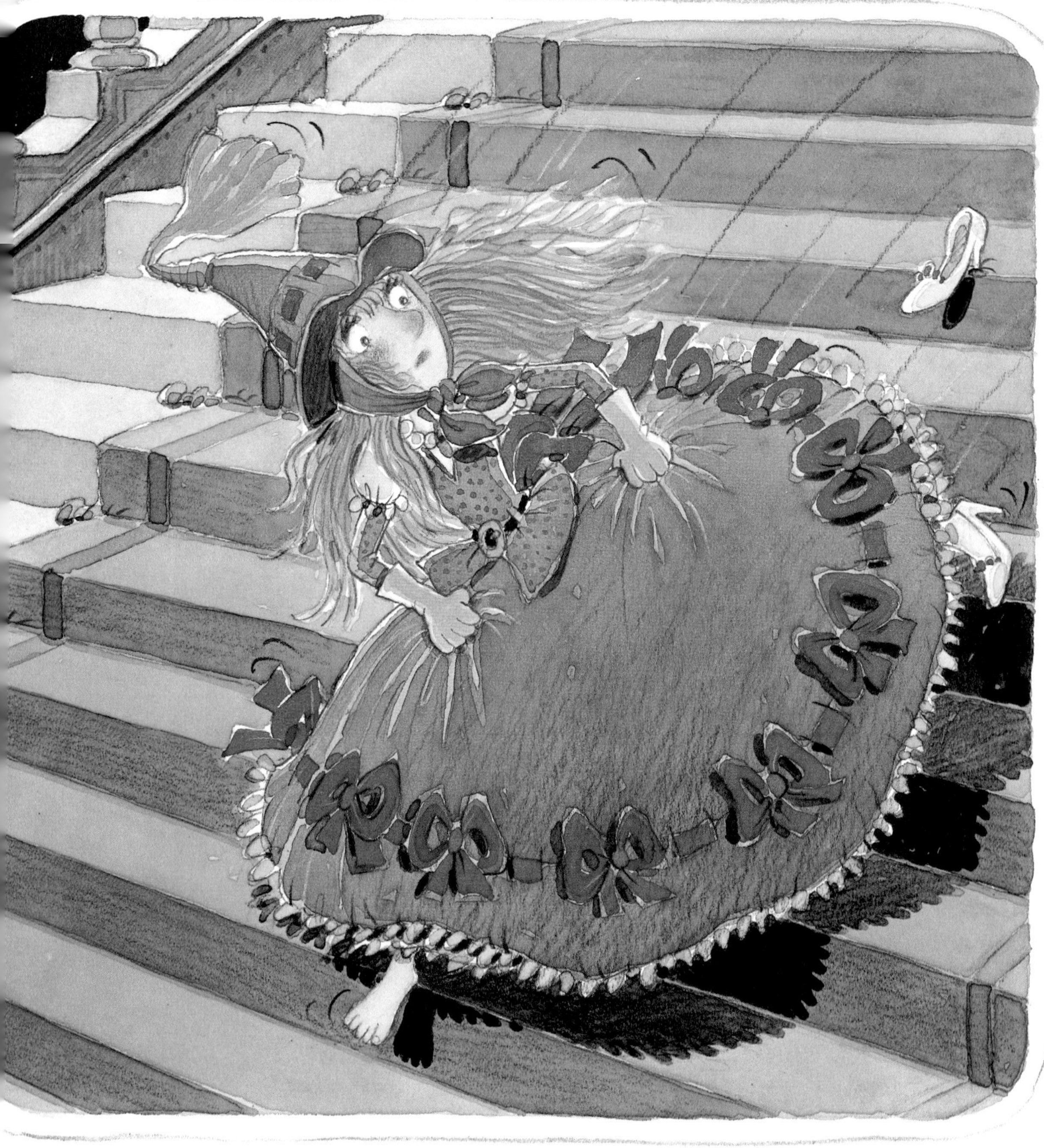

At once he ordered a messenger to search for the one who had lost the slipper. It was proclaimed throughout the land that the owner of the slipper would marry the prince.

What excitement there was! At every house, each lady tried to shove her foot into the tiny shoe. But, alas, no one could.

Finally, the messenger arrived at the house of Cinderella and her stepsisters.

"You have come to the right place," said Cinderella's stepmother. "The slipper belongs to one of my daughters."

The two sisters took turns trying to squeeze their feet into the slipper. They pushed and shoved, but it was no use. "You might as well give up," said the messenger in disgust. Still they kept trying.

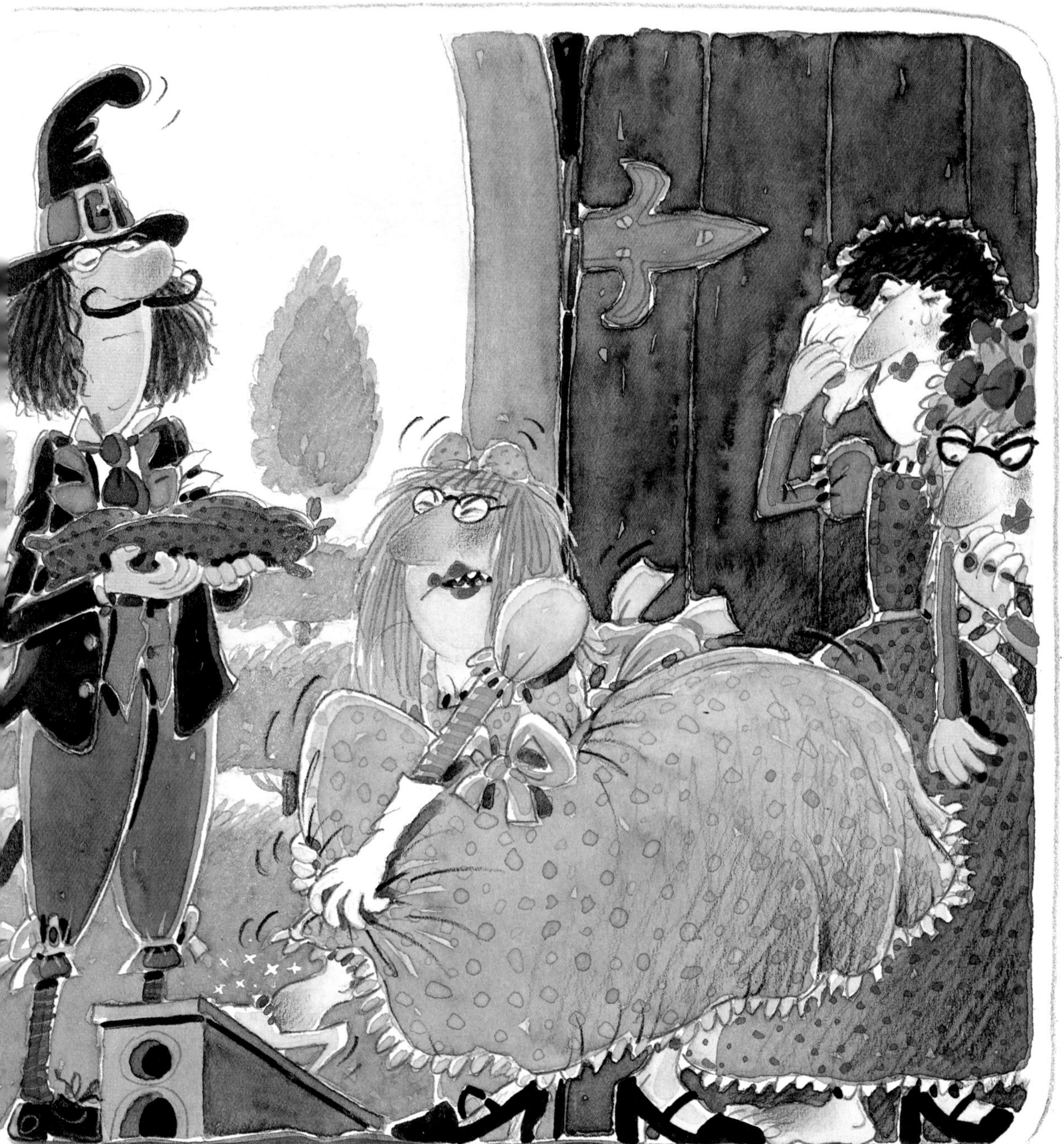

Now it happened that Cinderella came by on her way to the kitchen.

"Who is that?" asked the messenger.

"Oh, she is just a servant," said the stepmother. "The slipper could not be hers."

"All ladies must try on the slipper," said the messenger. "The prince has ordered it."

Cinderella's heart beat quickly as the messenger kneeled in front of her with the slipper. He slipped the shoe easily onto her foot. There was no doubt that she was the owner.

"It is you!" cried the messenger.

"Impossible!" screamed the stepsisters.

"How dare you try to fool the prince!" said the messenger to the stepsisters and their mother.

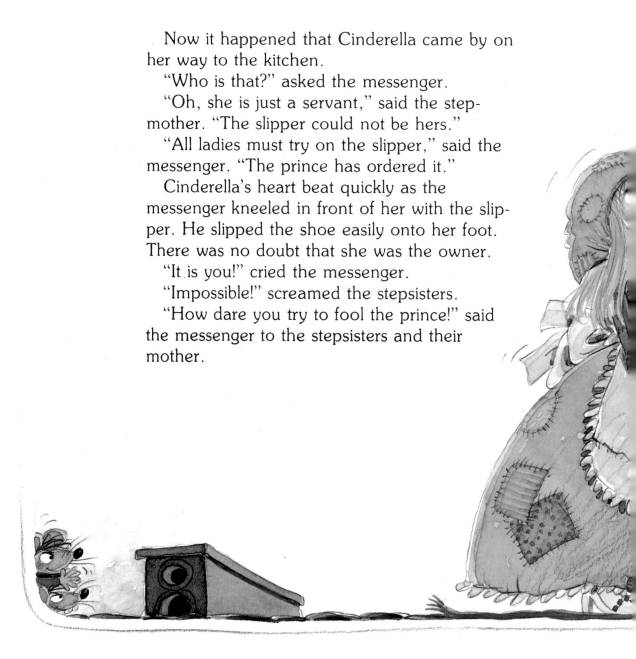

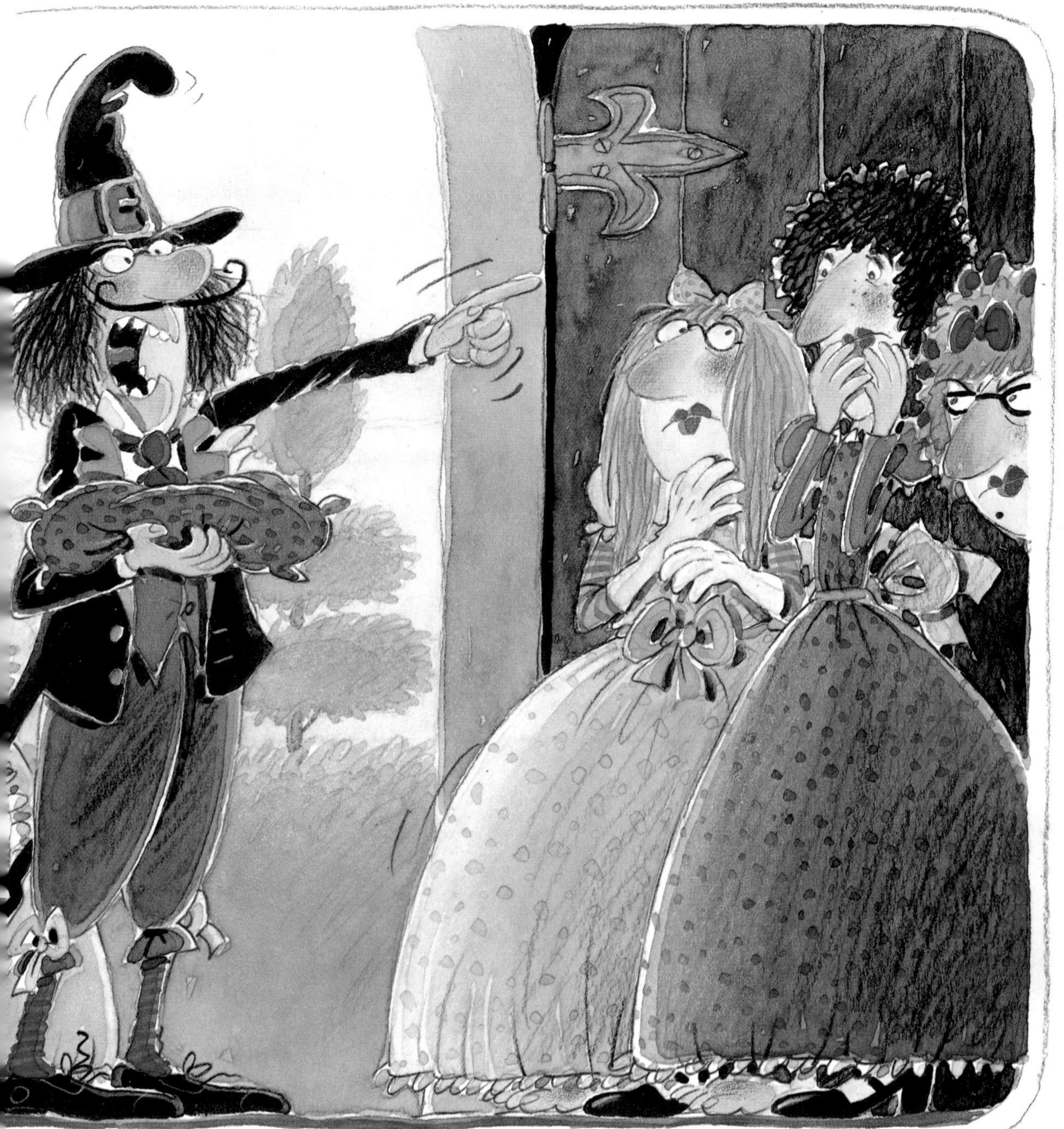

"Oh please don't punish them!" said Cinderella. "They are my family. I know that deep down they can't be as bad as they seem."

But the messenger ordered the three women to leave the kingdom until they had changed their ways.

Two months later, Cinderella and the prince were married in a joyful celebration. It is said that the train of Cinderella's wedding dress was carried by all the birds of the forest, the only friends she'd had in her days of sorrow.

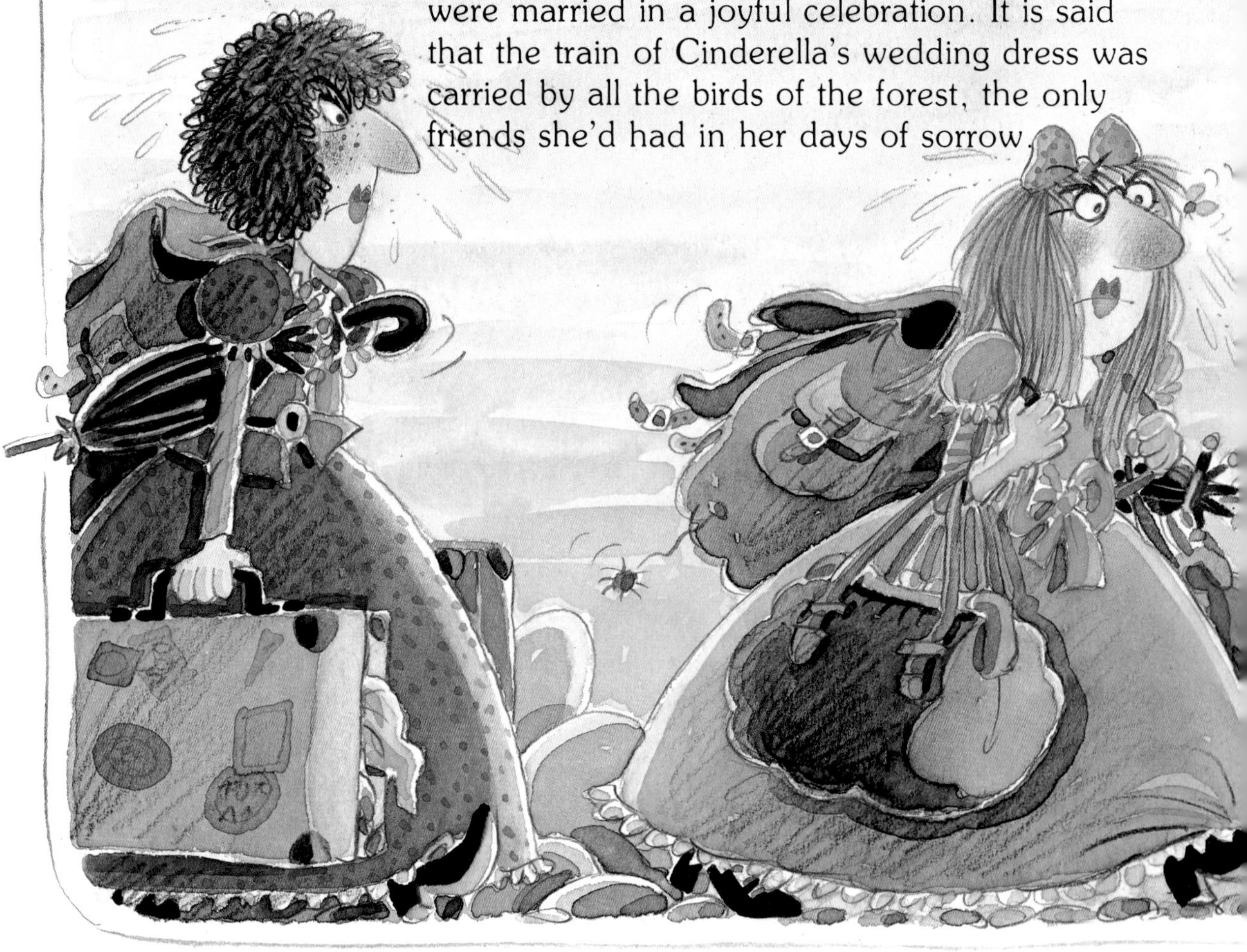

In time, the stepmother and her daughters came to regret all they had done. They returned and begged Cinderella to forgive them. Of course, Cinderella welcomed them with open arms, and from that day on, they all lived happily in the kingdom.

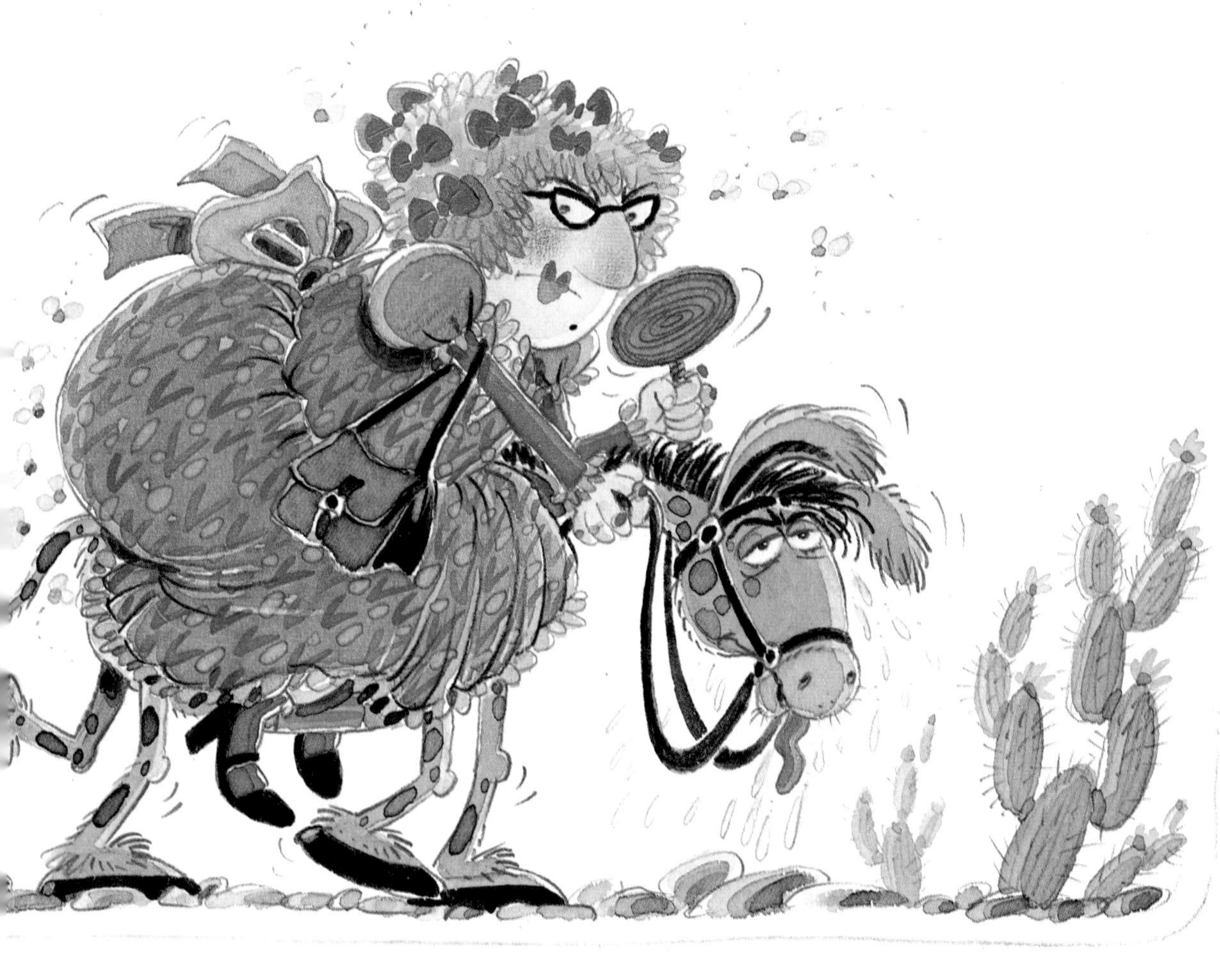